Making Roti

Written by Megan Borgert-Spaniol

Illustrated by Lisa Hunt

**GRL Consultant Diane Craig,
Certified Literacy Specialist**

Lerner Publications ◆ Minneapolis

Note from a GRL Consultant
This Pull Ahead leveled book has been carefully designed for beginning readers. A team of guided reading literacy experts has reviewed and leveled the book to ensure readers pull ahead and experience success.

Lerner Publications
An imprint of Lerner Publishing Group, Inc.
241 First Avenue North
Minneapolis, MN 55401 USA

For reading levels and more information, look up this title at www.lernerbooks.com.

Main body text set in Mikado 24/41
Typeface provided by Hannes von Doehren.

The images in this book are used with the permission of: Lisa Hunt

Library of Congress Cataloging-in-Publication Data

Names: Borgert-Spaniol, Megan, 1989– author. | Hunt, Lisa (Lisa Jane), 1973– illustrator.
Title: Making roti / written by Megan Borgert-Spaniol ; illustrated by Lisa Hunt.
Description: Minneapolis : Lerner Publications, [2023] | Series: My world (Pull ahead readers. Fiction) | Includes index. | Audience: Ages 4–7. | Audience: Grades K–1. | Summary: "Sundar makes roti with his mom. Includes leveled text and illustrations. Pairs with the nonfiction title We All Need Food"— Provided by publisher.
Identifiers: LCCN 2022008712 (print) | LCCN 2022008713 (ebook) | ISBN 9781728475899 (lib. bdg.) | ISBN 9781728478814 (pbk.) | ISBN 9781728483665 (eb pdf)
Subjects: LCSH: Readers (Primary) | LCGFT: Readers (Publications)
Classification: LCC PE1119.2 .B6749 2023 (print) | LCC PE1119.2 (ebook) | DDC 428.6/2— dc23/eng/20220310

LC record available at https://lccn.loc.gov/2022008712
LC ebook record available at https://lccn.loc.gov/2022008713

Manufactured in the United States of America
1 – CG – 12/15/22

Table of Contents

Making Roti

Sundar learns how to
make roti.
"Roti is a flat bread,"
said his mom.

Sundar makes the dough.

Sundar rolls out the dough.

His mom cooks the dough.

"The roti is done!"
said Sundar's mom.
"It looks good."

"Yes!" said Sundar.

"The roti is very good."

What are your favorite foods?

Did You See It?

bowl   **dough**   **roti**

Index